Books vs. Looks

★ Also by ★
Debbie Dadey

MERMAID TALES

BOOK 1: *TROUBLE AT TRIDENT ACADEMY*

BOOK 2: *BATTLE OF THE BEST FRIENDS*

BOOK 3: *A WHALE OF A TALE*

BOOK 4: *DANGER IN THE DEEP BLUE SEA*

BOOK 5: *THE LOST PRINCESS*

BOOK 6: *THE SECRET SEA HORSE*

BOOK 7: *DREAM OF THE BLUE TURTLE*

BOOK 8: *TREASURE IN TRIDENT CITY*

BOOK 9: *A ROYAL TEA*

BOOK 10: *A TALE OF TWO SISTERS*

BOOK 11: *THE POLAR BEAR EXPRESS*

BOOK 12: *WISH UPON A STARFISH*

BOOK 13: *THE CROOK AND THE CROWN*

BOOK 14: *TWIST AND SHOUT*

Coming Soon

BOOK 16: *FLOWER GIRL DREAMS*

Mermaid Tales

★ Debbie Dadey ★

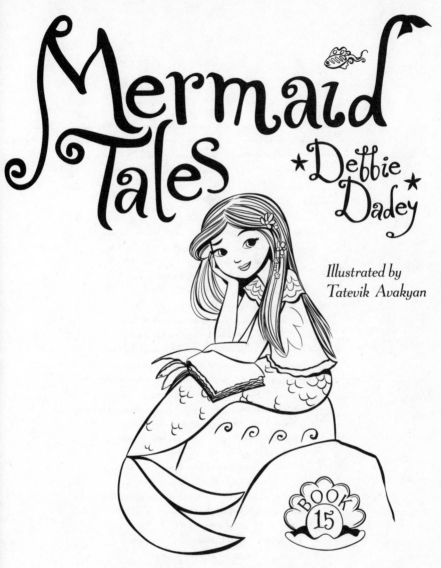

Illustrated by
Tatevik Avakyan

BOOK 15

Books vs. Looks

ALADDIN

NEW YORK   LONDON   TORONTO   SYDNEY   NEW DELHI

ALADDIN

An imprint of Simon & Schuster Children's Publishing Division

1230 Avenue of the Americas, New York, NY 10020

This Aladdin hardcover edition September 2016

Text copyright © 2016 by Debbie Dadey

Illustrations copyright © 2016 by Tatevik Avakyan

Also available in an Aladdin paperback edition.

All rights reserved, including the right of reproduction in whole or in part in any form.

ALADDIN is a trademark of Simon & Schuster, Inc.,

and related logo is a registered trademark of Simon & Schuster, Inc.

For information about special discounts for bulk purchases,

please contact Simon & Schuster Special Sales at 1-866-506-1949

or business@simonandschuster.com.

The Simon & Schuster Speakers Bureau can bring authors to your live event.

For more information or to book an event contact the

Simon & Schuster Speakers Bureau at 1-866-248-3049

or visit our website at www.simonspeakers.com.

Series designed by Karin Paprocki

Jacket designed by Karina Granda

The text of this book was set in Belucian Book.

Manufactured in the United States of America 0816 FFG

2 4 6 8 10 9 7 5 3 1

Library of Congress Control Number 2016944860

ISBN 978-1-4814-4082-0 (hc)

ISBN 978-1-4814-4081-3 (pbk)

ISBN 978-1-4814-4083-7 (eBook)

To Ava and her grandmother,

Karen Thurby Browder

★ ★ ★ ★

Acknowledgments

To Becky Dadey and her friend Kiki Mullikin, a real live Kiki!

Cast of Characters

Shelly

Echo

Kiki

Pearl

Rocky

Contents

A Special Letter

KIKI CORAL WAS SWIMMING to her dorm room after school one Friday when she felt a tap on her shoulder.

"Miss Coral," Madame Hippocampus announced. "You have a letter."

"Thanks," Kiki said as Madame handed

her a kelp envelope. Kiki smiled as she raced down the Trident Academy hallway. She bumped into a mergirl from her third-grade class.

"Watch out, for shark's sake!" Pearl Swamp snapped.

"Sorry," Kiki said, still clutching her letter. Her heart pounded in excitement. Kiki loved getting notes from her family in the Eastern Oceans. It made going to school so far away, in the Western Oceans, a little easier.

She soared through her doorway and swam straight to her killer-whale skeleton bed. Once she had curled her purple tail among the gray heron feathers, Kiki ripped open the letter.

★ 2 ★

Dear Kiki,

Hi! How is school? I wish I could go 2
Trident 2.

Guess what? My friends started a book
club! We are reading a scary book.
I will show it 2 u when u get home!

Miss u,

Yuta

Kiki read the letter twice and blinked back a tear. Her brother Yuta was a year younger than she was. She had been very close to him ever since they were small fry. Now that she went to school so far away, she really missed him.

Kiki glanced around her dorm room. Rainbow-colored jellyfish lamps hung from the curved ceiling, and a small waterfall tinkled gently in a corner. One whole wall glittered with plankton. A magnificent coral reef made up another wall. Kiki knew she was lucky to have such a fin-tastic space all to herself. At home her brothers had to share bedrooms.

But living all by herself could be lonely. Sometimes she wished she had someone to talk to. Weekends were the worst, because her best friends, Echo and Shelly, usually spent those evenings with their families. Many students who lived in the dorms also left to visit relatives.

At least she had plenty of books to read! Kiki looked at her tall rock bookcase and smiled. She had read every book on her shelf over and over. Reading stories always helped her feel less lonesome.

Kiki read Yuta's letter one more time before hopping on her tail with excitement. Even though Yuta was far away, he had given her a mer-velous idea!

Dr. Bottom

THE FOLLOWING MONDAY, Kiki couldn't wait to tell her merfriends about her idea. She had read in a book that humans had a device that allowed them to talk to people far away. Kiki wished she had one of those.

"Where are they?" Kiki tapped her purple tail on the classroom floor. If Shelly and Echo didn't swim in soon, they would be tardy. Their teacher, Mrs. Karp, was already at the front of the class. Just as the conch sounded to start the school day, Shelly, Echo, and a merboy named Rocky swooshed into the room.

Mrs. Karp raised a green eyebrow at the almost-late arrivals before starting her lesson. "Class, today we will begin a new area of study. Who can tell me about symbiosis?"

"I know! I know!" Rocky called out. "That's where you bang two shiny things together to make a really loud noise."

"Not quite," Mrs. Karp said. "Symbiosis

★ 7 ★

is when two different creatures live together in the same environment."

Kiki raised her hand. She remembered her father talking about that last year, before she had come to Trident Academy. "Don't the clown fish and the anemone do that?"

Mrs. Karp smiled and slapped her white tail on the classroom floor. "That's exactly right. It is a type of symbiosis called mutualism. Each one helps the other. The clown fish gets a safe home, and in return it cleans the anemone and even makes waste for it to eat."

Pearl gagged and twisted her pearl necklace. "That's disgusting!"

Mrs. Karp shrugged. "That's science. Today we have a special guest who will tell us more about different symbiotic relationships. Students, please welcome Dr. Bottom."

Kiki knew that Dr. Bottom usually taught fourth grade, but he sometimes switched with other teachers to teach science, his favorite subject.

"Good morning, Dr. Bottom," the merstudents said together. Rocky snickered when he said the science teacher's last name, but a quick look from Mrs. Karp silenced him.

"GOOD MORNING, CLASS!" Dr. Bottom shouted.

Kiki almost fell out of her chair. She quickly figured out that Dr. Bottom was hard of hearing. Over the next two hours he screamed his lesson about three different types of symbiotic relationships: mutualism, commensalism, and parasitism. Kiki tried to pay attention, but her mind kept wandering to her great idea.

When Dr. Bottom was finally finished, Kiki raced to the cafeteria for lunch. She just hoped her friends would love her idea too.

3

Club Flub

KIKI LOADED HER LUNCH tray with candy-stripe flatworms and warty frog-fish fritters and hurried to her usual spot at a table in the corner of the cafeteria. Her heart was pounding as she tapped her fingers on the gold Trident Academy logo in the center of the table.

Echo sat down with a giggle. "Guess what I read in a *MerStyle* magazine?" she said. "Princess Corissa eloped!"

"What does that mean?" Shelly asked as she slid into her seat. Her long red hair floated around her face.

"It's when merfolk swim away to get married," Echo explained.

"I heard that Mr. Fangtooth's wedding is in just a few weeks," Shelly told them before taking a bite of her fritter. Mr. Fangtooth was the grumpy cafeteria worker at their school. The girls had actually found a letter that had reunited him with his long-lost love.

"A wedding!" said Echo. "That is so romantic. I hope—"

"Guess what? I have the best idea ever!" Kiki blurted suddenly. She didn't mean to interrupt Echo, but she really couldn't wait any longer.

Echo and Shelly stared at Kiki in surprise. "What in the ocean is it?" Echo asked.

Kiki looked at her merfriends. They were so different from her. Shelly liked all kinds of sports, but mostly she loved playing Shell Wars, a game of tossing a shell around with long sticks. Echo loved sparkling things and tail-flipping on the school's dance and gymnastics team, the Tail Flippers. What if they hated her idea? There was only one way to find out.

Kiki took a deep breath and told her friends all about Yuta's letter. "My brother joined a club," she finished. "It gave me the idea to form one here at school, too."

"Splashing good!" Echo squealed. "We could start a human studies club and learn more about people." Kiki knew that Echo was fascinated by anything to do with humans.

Shelly nodded. "A cave-exploring club would be wavy too."

Kiki shook her head. "That's not what I had in mind. I want to start a book club."

"That could be fun," Echo said. "What happens in a book club?"

"We pick a book to read every week, and then we talk about it—our favorite parts and what we liked or didn't like," Kiki explained. "I have to ask Miss Scylla for permission, but I'd like to have the first meeting in the library tomorrow."

Shelly slurped up a long flatworm before saying, "I'm willing to give a book club a try."

Just then, a mergirl named Wanda floated by with her tray of food. She stopped and smiled. "A book club? That sounds mer-velous. Can I join too?"

"Of course!" Kiki said. "Everyone's welcome."

Pearl splashed up to their table. "A club?" she sputtered, turning her pointy nose up in the water. "What are you talking about? Wanda, are you joining something without me?"

"I'm starting a book club here at Trident Academy," Kiki told Pearl. "And it is open to everyone. Do you want to join? We're hoping to have the first meeting tomorrow after school."

Wanda smiled. "Come on, Pearl! It sounds totally wavy!"

Pearl sniffed at Kiki. "Why would I want to join *your* club, when I can make my own that's a zillion times better?"

With that, Pearl swirled around and floated toward her own table. Wanda shrugged and followed her.

"Uh-oh!" Echo said. "I think Pearl is mad!"

Kiki had a sinking feeling in her stomach. She knew that when it came to Pearl, there was no telling what might happen next.

Clash of the Posters

THE NEXT MORNING KIKI left for school extra early, carrying a big kelp poster that she had made herself. She had stayed up very late making sure her handwriting was perfect. She'd even drawn some pictures of her favorite books on the poster.

Kiki planned to ask Mrs. Karp for permission to hang the poster next to her classroom's door. Kiki hoped everyone would see it and want to join in the book club fun.

But when Kiki floated into the front hallway of Trident Academy, she got a huge surprise. Several posters were already plastered all over the walls:

JOIN THE BEST CLUB EVER!
PEARL SWAMP'S BUBBLING
BEAUTY BUNCH!
TODAY AFTER SCHOOL IN
FINN AUDITORIUM
FREE FOOD FROM MERLIN'S!

Kiki's heart sank. Why would anyone want to join her book club when they could get free food at Pearl's beauty club? Kiki was so sad that she almost ripped her poster to shreds, but she didn't. Instead she swam into her classroom and asked Mrs. Karp if she could put up her poster. When Mrs. Karp agreed, Kiki found an empty spot to hang her sign. Compared to Pearl's many signs, Kiki thought her one poster looked very small.

"No wavy way!" Shelly said as she swam into the classroom. "Did you see Pearl's posters?"

"For shark's shake," Echo said, swimming in right after Shelly. Echo pushed back her curly dark hair. "What happened

in the front hallway? It looks like a whale threw up posters!"

"I think Pearl wants to make sure that everyone joins her club and not mine," Kiki said with a frown.

"That's so mean!" Echo frowned. "I'm going to tell Pearl that it was your idea first."

Kiki shook her head. "No, I don't mind. Her beauty club sounds different from my club anyhow." Truthfully the posters did hurt Kiki's feelings, but she didn't want her merfriends to know that. She didn't want them to think she was jealous of Pearl.

"A beauty club could be fun," Echo admitted. "But why does Pearl have to have it at the same time as your book club?"

"I would change the day of our meeting, but today is the only time that all of us are free," Kiki explained.

On Mondays, Shelly often had Shell Wars practice. On Wednesdays, Echo usually practiced with the Tail Flippers. Kiki had vision lessons with Madame Hippocampus every Thursday. (Kiki was one of the few mermaids who could see the future.) The only school days left were Tuesdays and Fridays, and Kiki knew that on most Fridays both Shelly and Echo spent time with their families.

Shelly put her arm around Kiki. "Don't

worry about Pearl," she said. "Your club will still be the best club ever."

"How do you know that?" Kiki asked.

Shelly laughed. "Because we're going to be in it!"

The Best Club Ever

KIKI TRIED NOT TO THINK about Pearl's club that day, but it was hard not to. At lunchtime Pearl's table was crowded with mergirls. Kiki heard Pearl bragging loudly, "Besides the food from Merlin's, my mom is bringing fresh coconut milk and broiled blobfish burritos for snacks. And next week she promised to get some cuttlefish candy!"

The girls at Pearl's lunch table squealed with delight at the mention of this rare treat. Even Kiki loved cuttlefish candy. She looked at Shelly and Echo and knew they were thinking the same thing.

"You guys can join Pearl's club if you want. I won't mind," Kiki told them. She actually didn't want her friends to join the Bubbling Beauty Bunch. But she didn't want to stop them either.

"Don't be silly," Echo said. "We're your merfriends, and merfriends don't do that to friends."

Wanda swam up to Kiki and tapped

her on the shoulder. "I'm really sorry," Wanda said, "but I can't go to your meeting after school. Pearl told me that I have to join her club or she won't be merfriends with me anymore." Wanda hung her head.

Kiki tried to smile. "I understand."

Wanda nodded and rushed away.

"Pearl makes me so mad sometimes!" Shelly snapped.

"Don't let it make your tail spin," Kiki said. "It doesn't bother me."

But it did. Kiki had seventeen brothers, so she was used to not always getting her way, but sometimes Pearl just made Kiki bubbling mad.

Suddenly an announcement boomed

over the conch shell from Headmaster Hermit. "Will Pearl Swamp—or the merstudent who put posters all over the school without permission—please come to my office?"

All eyes turned to Pearl, whose face became bright red. She frowned as she floated out of her seat and swam past Kiki's table. "You're probably happy that I'm getting sent to Headmaster Hermit's office," Pearl hissed. "You just want to ruin my club!"

Kiki's long, dark hair swirled in the water as she shook her head. "No, I don't!" she cried.

But Pearl was already out the lunchroom door.

All afternoon, Pearl glared at Kiki during Mrs. Karp's lessons. In art class Pearl even stuck her tongue out at Kiki while the merstudents were drawing pictures of symbiotic relationships!

As she passed by Kiki's art table, Pearl whispered, "Headmaster Hermit told me to take down the posters, but I'm not in real trouble. And my beauty club is going to be the best ever. No one will want to join your silly book group."

Kiki put her hand over her mouth. Her tummy felt like it was doing tail flips. She didn't want to start a club war with Pearl! But that seemed to be exactly what Pearl was doing.

Finally the school day was over. That meant it was time for Kiki's very first book club meeting!

Kiki, Shelly, and Echo sat in the library with a stack of kelp and stone books on the table in front of them. They were the only students there. Kiki didn't know whether to feel disappointed or excited, especially when she heard cheers coming from Finn Auditorium, where Pearl's Bubbling Beauty Bunch was meeting for the first time.

The librarian floated up to the three mergirls. "Your book club is a wonderful idea," Miss Scylla told them. "Let me know if I can do anything to—"

Miss Scylla was interrupted by a

roar of laughter from the auditorium. Kiki cringed but smiled at the librarian. "Thanks for suggesting these books," she said. Miss Scylla nodded and floated back to her desk.

Echo picked up a brightly colored book with a human on the cover. "Which story should we read first?" she asked.

"Hmm," Kiki said. "It should be one that we all like."

Echo frowned. "But what if we can't agree?"

"Maybe we each choose one book? Kiki, you can start, since the club was your idea," Shelly suggested.

"That is a splashing good plan," Kiki agreed.

"Shouldn't our club have a name?" Echo asked.

"Mer-velous suggestion!" Kiki exclaimed. "What should we call it?"

Shelly giggled. "Well, you know how we've been studying symbiotic relationships and how some creatures work together?"

"Sure," Echo said. "But what does that have to do with a book club?"

"Since we all get friendship from one another, we could name our club the Mutualism Book Club," Shelly suggested.

Kiki smiled just as another loud roar of laughter came from the auditorium. She didn't know how long the Mutualism Book Club would last, but for now she was happy.

6

Floating with Style

THE NEXT MORNING ROCKY, Adam, Morgan, Wanda, and Kiki were the first ones in Mrs. Karp's classroom.

"I ate so many broiled blobfish burritos at Pearl's club yesterday, I burped blobs all night!" Rocky told Adam.

Kiki looked at Rocky in surprise. "You went to a Bubbling Beauty Bunch meeting?" she asked.

Rocky shrugged. "Free snacks! And I was hungry."

"Me too," Adam said. "I didn't even care that Pearl put ribbons in my hair. That coconut milk was tail-kicking! I think it's even better than the Big Rock Café's."

"Yeah, b-but Pearl was being b-bossy!" Morgan complained. "She said Tyra B-Baybanks, the fashion expert, insists that f-f-fin decorations are shelltacular. Then she told us since it's her c-c-club we have to d-d-do things her way." Morgan held up her sparkling orange tail. Kiki noticed that Wanda's red tail glittered as well.

Rocky smacked his plain brown tail on the classroom floor. "Well, I don't care what Pearl says, I'm not wearing jewel anemones!"

"No cuttlefish candy for you then," Adam teased, although Kiki noticed that Adam wasn't wearing fin jewelry either.

"What book is your club reading?" Wanda asked Kiki.

Kiki smiled. "Well, first we're reading *Dolphins Don't Play Shell Wars*. But we're taking turns choosing which book to read."

"Oh, that sounds so much better than what Pearl read to us," Morgan told her just as Shelly and Echo swam into the room.

"What's that?" Shelly asked.

"She read aloud from the fashion section of *MerStyle* magazine," Wanda told them.

Adam put his hands on his hips and grunted. "Then she made us float with style."

"How do you float with style?" Kiki asked.

Rocky jerked his tail back and forth in a silly way. "Don't I look beautiful?" he said, batting his eyelashes.

Kiki, Echo, and Shelly burst out laughing. "Maybe Pearl's club should be called the Parasite Beauty Bunch, not the Bubbling Beauty Bunch," Echo said. "She's forcing everyone to do what she wants!"

Rocky snorted. "Pearl the Parasite! That's the perfect name for her."

Kiki frowned. Even though Pearl could be mean, it wasn't nice to make fun of her.

Kiki started to tell Rocky that Pearl was not a parasite. After all, she was giving them great snacks in exchange for their club membership; that was an example of mutualism. But before she could open her mouth, Wanda floated over to Kiki and whispered, "Do you think I could read your club's book too?"

"Of course," Kiki said. "Miss Scylla has several more copies in the library."

Wanda smiled. "Mer-velous! Just don't tell Pearl."

"Don't tell Pearl what?" Pearl said from the doorway.

"Um, n-nothing," Wanda said. "I was just asking Kiki about her club, and—"

"You're trying to join Kiki's club instead of mine!" Pearl accused her.

"No," Kiki explained. "Wanda just wondered what book we were reading."

"Wanda, you traitor!" Pearl snapped.

Wanda looked up in horror as a red-faced Pearl swam into the classroom.

"Pearl," Wanda cried. "I'm so sorry!"

"Are you my friend or not?" Pearl asked angrily.

"Of course," Wanda said.

"Then why are you deserting me for Kiki's club?" Pearl demanded.

"I just want to be a member of both clubs," Wanda explained with a frown.

But Pearl refused to even look at Wanda as Mrs. Karp started the day's lesson.

Friend Stealer!

T LUNCHTIME KIKI, SHELLY, and Echo swam up to Pearl, who was eating at her usual lunch table. Wanda wasn't sitting with her.

"Why did you yell at Wanda like that?" Kiki asked Pearl. "You hurt Wanda's feelings, and now she thinks that you don't want to be friends with her."

"Me?" Pearl sputtered. "I'm not the one who's stealing friends!"

Kiki shook her head. "I'm not stealing friends," she said. "I just wanted to have a book club like my brother has. I didn't want a club war."

"Sweet seaweed, Pearl!" Echo said. "The whole club thing was Kiki's idea in the first place. *You're* the one who stole it from her!"

Pearl's face turned pink and then bright red. She looked like she was ready to explode.

Luckily, Wanda whirled into the cafeteria. She tapped Pearl on the shoulder. "Look at what came in the mail!" she said.

Wanda showed Pearl two sparkling bracelets. They were a perfect matched set. "I ordered one for each of us a long time ago," Wanda explained.

"You did?" Pearl said, clearly surprised.

"Hey, look," Rocky said as he swam by to turn in his lunch tray. "It's barracuda bait."

"It is not," Pearl snapped, although barracudas do like shiny things. "It is a wonderful gift from my best pal."

Wanda and Pearl hugged. Kiki was glad the two merfriends were back together. But she still didn't understand why Pearl was jealous of her. Was it because Wanda had once been Kiki's roommate?

After lunch Mrs. Karp's class had a spelling lesson. Kiki could barely concentrate on how to spell "mutualism." She was still in shock over the way Pearl had accused her of trying to steal Wanda. She was glad when snack time came and she was able to put Pearl and Wanda out of her mind.

But Pearl hadn't forgotten. She floated beside Kiki's desk and hissed, "You may not have wanted a competition, Kiki Coral, but you've got one! Maybe Wanda thought about joining your silly club, but no one else will. Just wait and see!"

That night, as Kiki nestled into the feathers of her bed, she tried to read *Dolphins Don't Play Shell Wars*, but she kept losing her place. She couldn't help wondering what in the ocean Pearl was planning next.

Pearl's Prizes

THURSDAY MORNING, AS SHE entered the school's front hallway, Kiki found out. Huge kelp banners hung on every wall!

Win Fin-tastic, One-of-a-Kind Prizes

at Pearl's Bubbling Beauty Bunch!

Shelly and Echo floated up to Kiki. "Is she really going to give merkids prizes just for showing up?" Shelly asked, shaking her head.

Kiki shrugged. "It sure looks like it."

"What kind of prizes?" Echo wondered.

"Well, it is Pearl," Shelly answered. "So, there's no telling."

Pearl lived in the fanciest house in all of Trident City, and she always seemed to get whatever she wanted.

"I guess we'll find out next week," Kiki said with a sigh. "If you guys want to go to her club meeting, I'll understand."

"No wavy way!" Shelly said.

"Besides, I really like the book you picked," Echo told Kiki.

"Me too," Shelly said. "Did you get to the funny part where they're in the cafeteria?"

Kiki held up her hand. "Not yet! Don't tell me—I want to read it for myself."

The following Tuesday, Kiki, Echo, and Shelly met at their usual spot in the library for book club. Echo had just told them all about her favorite part in *Dolphins Don't Play Shell Wars* when a parade of merkids floated past the door. Each carried a prize. Some had large shells or new merclothes, while others lugged funny-shaped objects that could only be from humans.

Kiki knew how much Echo loved human objects. "I wish I could hand out prizes too," Kiki told her merfriends.

Shelly pushed her long red hair out of her face and frowned. "For shark's sake! You don't need to give us prizes. Pearl is just trying to buy club members."

Echo smiled. "And anyway," she said, "merfriends are the best prize!"

A Sweet Surprise

AT THE END OF THEIR MEET-
ing, Kiki, Echo, and Shelly
made a dolphin craft to go
along with their book. Shelly stood back to
look at her creation. She had molded it from
clay that Echo's sister had donated. "I think
I'm going to name my dolphin Penelope."

"Why Penelope?" Echo asked, wiping her clay-covered hands on a piece of kelp.

"I heard that name once and always liked it," Shelly said. "If I could change my name, it would be Penelope."

"I'd be Millicent," Echo said. "What about you, Kiki?"

Kiki had never thought about it. "I like my name just the way it is, but I am sorry these treats aren't as fancy as Pearl's," she said putting some snacks on the table. "Still, I think they're yummy." Kiki wished her mother had sent her some cuttlefish candy in her most recent package from home.

"You know I love sea cucumbers," Shelly said, popping two of the crunchy treats into her mouth. "Plus, I need to eat something healthy before my Shell Wars game."

"And the Tail Flippers are performing at the game too," Echo said, before taking the last sip of her kelp drink. "Thanks for making this a short meeting."

"You guys go ahead," Kiki told her mer-friends. "Good luck with the game! I'll stick around and clean this up."

"Are you sure?" Shelly said.

Kiki nodded. "It's only a few crumbs, but I don't want Miss Scylla to get mad at us. It's nice of her to let us use the library for our meetings."

"Thanks!" Shelly said. "Coach Barnacle gets upset when we're late."

"So does Coach Sarah," Echo agreed. Sarah SeaLion was Coach Barnacle's assistant. The two coached both the Tail Flippers and the Shell Wars team.

After her merfriends left, Kiki hummed a song to herself as she wiped off the marble table. The library was one of her favorite places. There was something satisfying about the neat rows of kelp and stone books. The soft glow of the jellyfish on the chandeliers lit up the beautiful ceiling, giving the room a cozy feeling.

"No wavy way! You're still here!" Pearl snapped from the doorway.

Kiki looked up in surprise. "I was just cleaning up. I think this is such a beautiful library, so I didn't want to leave it messy."

Pearl nodded. "I think it's lovely too. I was mad when you beat me to it for your book club. But there are so many people in *my* club that the library is probably too small anyway."

"Congratulations," Kiki told Pearl. "Your club is a big hit. I saw lots of merkids leaving with prizes earlier."

"Well, some of the merboys turned over the snack table and made a huge mess!" Pearl huffed. "Then they didn't even help clean it up! And lots of merkids left after they got their prizes." She paused, then asked, "How is your little club going?"

Kiki shrugged. "It's small, but that's okay. Sometimes I get lonely here at Trident Academy. I really miss my parents and my brothers. Having the club helps."

"Why are you lonely?" Pearl asked. "You have Shelly and Echo for merfriends."

"That's true, and they are great mer-buddies," Kiki agreed. "But it's not the same as having your family around. Plus, I don't have a roommate, so the evenings get pretty quiet when everyone goes to their own homes and rooms. That's why I love books."

She didn't mention the fact that Pearl was the reason Kiki didn't have a roommate. At the beginning of the school year, Wanda had been Kiki's roommate. But Wanda told Pearl that Kiki's killer whale bed was creepy, so Pearl got Kiki kicked out of Wanda's room!

"I guess I didn't think about that," Pearl said. "So that's why you started the book club? You were lonely?"

Kiki nodded. "I wasn't trying to steal Wanda."

Pearl was quiet for a while, which Kiki thought was strange. Then Pearl asked, "Do you want a piece of cuttlefish candy? I only have one left."

Kiki smiled. "Thanks! That would be nice."

After Pearl left, Kiki crunched on the candy. She couldn't believe that after declaring a club war, Pearl had given her a treat. Kiki wondered what Pearl would do next.

Fashion Forward

THE NEXT MORNING KIKI arrived at school to find Shelly and Echo floating in front of Pearl's latest poster.

TRIDENT ACADEMY FASHION SHOW

Next Friday After School

Pearl's Bubbling Beauty Bunch invites

all interested merkids to participate.

Cost: One shell to attend.

Will help a good cause.

Rehearsal this Friday after school

in Finn Auditorium.

"A fashion show? Oh, that sounds fun!" Echo squealed. Then she slapped her hand over her mouth and looked at Kiki. "Sorry."

Kiki shrugged. "It actually does sound pretty shelltacular. Maybe we should all take part in it."

"You wouldn't mind being in Pearl's fashion show?" Echo asked.

"Of course not," Kiki said, pointing to the poster. "Both the rehearsal and the

★ 60 ★

show are on Fridays, so they won't conflict with our book club. Plus, it says right here that all proceeds will help a good cause."

"What about you, Shelly?" Echo asked.

Kiki knew fashion wasn't exactly Shelly's favorite thing. "I guess I could give it a try," Shelly said.

"Fin-tastic!" Echo said. The three friends swam into Mrs. Karp's classroom, where the whole class was buzzing about Pearl's newest poster. Every mergirl and a few merboys wanted to be in the fashion show.

On Friday at the rehearsal, Finn Auditorium was filled with merkids. Pearl put Rocky and a few other third graders in charge of the music and decorations.

"I-I love the dress I'm wearing," said Morgan. "Can I w-wear it in the show?"

"Mmm," Pearl said, glancing at Morgan and ignoring her stuttering. "It *is* a pretty dress, but wouldn't you rather wear one from MerLinda's Boutique? They are lending us some clothes to wear." MerLinda's was the fanciest dress shop in Trident City.

Morgan squealed. "That sounds mer-velous!"

"Shelltacular! We can go there tomor-row." Pearl turned to Wanda. "Do you want to write up a description of every outfit for Headmaster Hermit to read aloud?" Pearl asked.

"You bet!" Wanda said.

Kiki couldn't believe that Pearl had gotten Headmaster Hermit to agree to be the master of ceremonies for the event.

Kiki tapped Pearl on the shoulder and asked, "What do you think of this outfit for the show?" Kiki twirled around, modeling something her grandmother had given her.

Pearl twisted her long pearl necklace in her fingers and nodded. "That is perfect!"

Kiki grinned.

On the night of the show, Finn Auditorium was sparkling with plankton and balloonfish. The merkids gathered backstage, dressed in their elegant clothes. As she peeked through the curtain, Kiki had to admit she was excited. She was also a bit nervous about all the people she saw floating into the auditorium. It was a big crowd, and Kiki didn't like most big things.

"All right, merboys and mergirls," Pearl announced, clapping her hands. "This is it! Remember to smile and act natural." Pearl's blond hair was in a fancy updo that looked like it might fall over at any minute.

Kiki looked at the merkids in line. All the third graders were dressed in beautiful outfits with sparkling plankton bows in their hair.

"You look splashing good," Shelly said, admiring Kiki's outfit. "I've never seen anything so beautiful."

"Thanks! It's called a kimono," Kiki explained. "It is an old tradition in the Eastern Oceans. My grandmother made this one. It took her two years!"

"Sweet seaweed!" Shelly exclaimed. "I can't imagine working on anything for that long!"

Kiki tightened her sash, or obi. "All the decorations make it really heavy to wear. I'm afraid I'll trip over my tail when I go onstage!"

Wanda looked even more frightened than Kiki felt. Kiki remembered when Wanda had starred in the school's play of *The Little Human*. Wanda had had terrible stage fright.

"I'm so scared that I think I'm going to throw up," Wanda said. "I can't go out there!"

Pearl shook her head. Her updo wiggled back and forth. "No, you're going to be fine. In fact, you and I will float out together."

Wanda looked grateful. "Really?"

"Of course," Pearl said. "Now, let's do this!"

Pearl stepped out onto the stage, pulling Wanda behind her. Kiki noticed they were both wearing their sparkling bracelets. Music blared as the show began.

Kiki gulped. Would she really be able to be a fashion model when it was her turn, or would she be the one to throw up onstage?

Runway Time!

"ARE YOU ALL RIGHT?" ECHO asked Kiki.

Kiki shook her head. "What if I do a tail flop right into the audience? Everyone will laugh at me!"

"You're not going to tumble down," Shelly

said. "And even if you did, it wouldn't be the end of the ocean."

"But you just said I wouldn't fall!" Kiki cried. She knew she wasn't making any sense, but she couldn't help herself. She had never been more jittery.

"I know! What if we all float out there together?" Echo suggested.

Shelly nodded. "We could go out as a group, and then each of us could swim forward and take a bow when Headmaster Hermit calls our name."

That didn't sound so hard. "O-okay. I can do that," Kiki agreed.

"After all, we are the Mutualism Book Club," Echo said with a giggle. "We have to stick together."

Shelly shook her head. "Today we are the Mutualistic Fashion Club! Let's go!"

As they floated out onto the stage, Kiki was shocked again by the huge crowd. It looked like the whole school as well as many citizens of Trident City were there.

Headmaster Hermit introduced Shelly and Echo. Then he said, "And now, we have Kiki Coral. She is wearing a delightful pink kimono from her native waters in the Eastern Oceans. It is embellished with hundreds of colorful crystal beads and lovely shells from the cayenne keyhole limpet in an amazing daisy coral pattern."

Kiki smiled as the audience clapped and cheered. She twirled around, grateful that she didn't trip and fall.

In fact, no one did. The whole fashion show went off without a hitch.

After every last merkid had taken their turn on the runway, Headmaster Hermit cleared his throat. "And now," he said, "Pearl Swamp has an announcement."

Pearl wiggled back onto the stage, her tall hairdo still in place. "Thank you so much for coming to our Bubbling Beauty Bunch Fashion Show. Could Miss Scylla please come onstage?"

There was a murmur in the audience as the librarian came forward. Rocky and Adam helped Pearl drag a large chest in

front of Miss Scylla. Kiki couldn't help giggling when she saw that Rocky wore a shirt that sparkled.

"This chest holds the shells we raised this afternoon," Pearl told everyone. "The Bubbling Beauty Bunch would like Miss Scylla to use these shells to buy new books for the Trident Academy library."

The entire audience clapped as Miss Scylla thanked Pearl and the rest of the club. "After all, books are our friends, even when we are lonely," Pearl said, winking at Kiki.

Kiki couldn't believe it. Would Pearl ever stop surprising her?

12

A Fin-tastic Finish

THAT NIGHT, BACK IN HER dorm room, Kiki started writing a letter to her brother Yuta.

Dear Yuta,

I miss Mom, Dad, and everyone else,

but I miss you most of all.

Guess what? I loved your idea

about the book club so much that

I started one here at Trident

Academy. A girl named Pearl also

started a beauty club.

Kiki held her orange sea pen over her letter. Should she tell Yuta how Pearl had tried to start a club war? Kiki decided not to. After all, in the end it was Pearl's idea to have a fashion show to raise money for the library.

"Kiki!" Wanda was suddenly in Kiki's doorway. "Come look!"

"What's wrong?" Kiki said.

"You aren't going to believe what Pearl's

done now!" Wanda said. She waved Kiki toward the hallway.

Kiki left her letter and swam with Wanda to the front entrance of Trident Academy. What had Pearl done this time? Had she rented a troupe of dancing dolphins for the next Bubbling Beauty Bunch meeting? Or maybe she'd hired a chef to prepare honeycomb worm scones or a merstylist to give everyone fancy haircuts. What if she got the most famous boy band in the ocean to perform? Kiki would love to see the Rays again herself.

But when Kiki and Wanda got to the front hallway, it was none of those things. Wanda pointed to a small sign by the door.

NOTICE:

PEARL'S BUBBLING BEAUTY

BUNCH IS NO MORE!

PLEASE JOIN KIKI CORAL'S

BOOK CLUB INSTEAD.

Kiki shook her head. Were her eyes playing tricks on her?

She looked at Wanda and asked, "Why?"

Wanda shrugged. "I don't know. I just saw the sign and came to tell you."

Kiki thought back to the library and how she'd told Pearl she was lonely. Could it be that Pearl just might have a heart after all?

"What are you going to do now?" Wanda asked.

Kiki smiled. "Right now, I'm going to finish a letter to my brother. I have a lot to tell him. And tomorrow, I'm going to give Pearl a big hug!"

Kiki's Guide to Starting a Book Club

★ ✦ ★

ASK A TEACHER OR PARENT if you can use a space for your club.

Ask your classmates to join.

You can even put up posters to let others know. Be nice and let everyone join.

Take turns picking the books to read or draw titles from a box.

Whoever chooses the book can bring a snack and organize a craft to match the book.

Everyone could bring questions about the book to the meeting.

It might be fun to name your group.

Everyone could read their favorite part of the book aloud, or explain why one character is their favorite.

An adult may want to help you. Be sure to get permission for whatever you do!

Pearl's Guide on How to Start a Bubbling Beauty Bunch Club

* ✦ *

ASK A TEACHER OR PARENT if you can use a space for your club.

You can even put up posters to let others know. Be nice and let everyone join. Be sure to ask permission to put up the posters!

Read beauty tips from *MerStyle* magazine like:

"A smile is the best addition to any outfit," Tyra Baybanks says.

Stacy Loggerhead tells us, "A mermaid should always shimmer!"

"Don't be afraid of bright colors. Have fun!"—Mackerel Jacobs

Get the best snacks you can. It would be great to take turns so one person doesn't have to do it all!

Try new hairstyles with ribbons.

Invite a fashion expert or clothing store owner to visit.

Name your group something fashion forward.

You might even want to have a fashion show with everyone's favorite outfit and give away the shells to a good cause.

An adult may want to help you, but be sure to get permission for whatever you do!

Scenes of Symbiotic Relationships

THE WHALE SHARK AND THE REMORA

by Shelly Siren

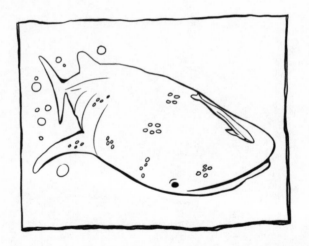

The scene I drew shows the big whale shark
and the small remora fish. Why doesn't the

whale shark eat the remora? The remora gets to eat scraps of food from the shark's meal, but it also cleans the shark's body. This type of symbiotic relationship is called mutualism.

THE MEAN BARNACLE AND THE POOR CRAB

by Echo Reef

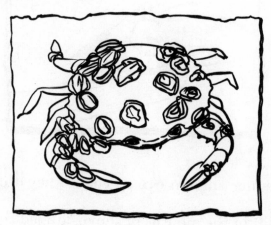

I drew a scene with mean barnacles hurting a crab. Because the barnacles hurt the crab, this is called parasitism. That's why I don't like barnacles.

CLEANER SHRIMP AND SHARP-FANGED EELS
by Rocky Ridge

Cleaner shrimp are so cool! They'll even swim in the mouths of sharp-fanged eels! I forgot what it's called, but both of them like it because they both get something out of it.

The shrimp get food and the eels get clean! Did I tell you I once had a cleaner shrimp clean my mouth? Oh, I remember. That type of relationship is called mutualism.

THE PORCELAIN CRAB AND THE ANEMONE

by Pearl Swamp

I did a report on porcelain crabs before, and I learned that they like to live around anemones. The porcelain crab coats itself with anemone snot so it won't get stung! Have you ever heard of anything so disgusting? Anyway, this is mutualism, because the crab keeps the anemone clean and the crab has a safe place to live.

GRAY WHALES AND BARNACLES
by Kiki Coral

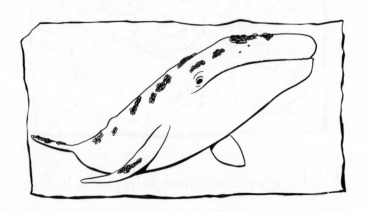

I decided to draw a scene showing a gray whale with barnacles for commensalism, a kind of symbiosis where only one creature gets something. Can you believe that sometimes one whale can have as many as one thousand barnacles? The barnacles are protected by the whale's body and get to enjoy the same food as the whale, but they usually don't hurt the whale.

The Mermaid Tales Song

REFRAIN:

Let the water roar

Deep down we're swimming along

Twirling, swirling, singing the mermaid song.

VERSE 1:

Shelly flips her tail

Racing, diving, chasing a whale

Twirling, swirling, singing the mermaid song.

VERSE 2:

Pearl likes to shine

Oh my Neptune, she looks so fine

Twirling, swirling, singing the mermaid song.

VERSE 3:

Shining Echo flips her tail

Backward and forward without fail

Twirling, swirling, singing the mermaid song.

VERSE 4:

Amazing Kiki

Far from home and floating so free

Twirling, swirling, singing the mermaid song.

Author's Note

BECAUSE I HAVE MOVED A lot, I know how Kiki feels. Sometimes it is hard to make friends in a strange place, but clubs are a great way to meet new people. Maybe you'd even like to start up a book club like Kiki or a beauty club like Pearl. If so, they have a few suggestions for you.

Have fun,
Debbie

P.S. Check out my website, debbiedadey.com, for fun mermaid fashion tips in *MerStyle* magazines and for ways to start a Mermaid Tales club.

Glossary

ANEMONE: This creature attaches itself to surfaces and grabs food with its stinging tentacles.

ATLANTIC MACKEREL: This fish has a torpedo-shaped body and can swim very fast.

BALLOONFISH: The porcupine fish is sometimes called a balloonfish or blowfish. When it is afraid it will swell up so that it looks like a spikey basketball.

BARNACLE: Adult barnacles spend their whole lives attached to rocks or another surface.

BARRACUDA: Barracudas like to eat shiny fish. In fact, they have been known to try to eat shiny things on divers!

BLOBFISH: The poor blobfish was once voted the world's ugliest creature. It looks like a blob! It lives in very deep waters near Australia.

CANDY-STRIPE FLATWORM: This flatworm is cream colored with reddish stripes and likes to live in rocky areas.

CAYENNE KEYHOLE LIMPET: If you ever see a pattern in the algae on rocks in or near the ocean, it could be the trail a limpet has left behind.

CLEANER SHRIMP: The scarlet skunk cleaner shrimp has red-and-white stripes down its back.

CLOWN FISH: Clown fish can be many colors, including yellow, orange, or black. They usually have white stripes or patches.

COCONUT: Coconuts are the round fruit of the palm tree. Inside the hard fruit is a seed, which is part solid and part milk. Sometimes coconuts fall into the ocean.

CONCH: Conchs have beautiful spiral shells. For years people have collected them, and now they are endangered.

CORAL: This creature lives in groups that fix themselves to the ocean floor. Daisy coral actually looks a bit like a daisy flower.

CUTTLEFISH: Cuttlefish are related to squids. They can change colors to hide themselves and squirt ink when afraid.

DOLPHIN: The Indo-Pacific humpback dolphin gets its name from the hump beneath its dorsal (back) fin.

GRAY HERON: This tall bird grabs fish out of the water with its long, sharp beak.

HONEYCOMB WORM: This little creature makes big tubes of sand that look like honeycombs.

JELLYFISH: There are many kinds of jellyfish, but the box jellyfish is the most dangerous. Its sting is extremely painful. It lives near Australia.

KELP: Kelp is large, brown seaweed.

KILLER WHALE: Killer whales are the biggest of the dolphins. They are also known as orcas.

LOGGERHEAD TURTLE: The loggerhead

turtle is the second largest marine turtle, after the leatherback.

ORANGE SEA PEN: This creature likes to live in the sand or mud and looks very much like an old-fashioned quill pen.

PLANKTON: Tiny creatures that float with the ocean currents and live near the surface are called plankton. Some plankton glow!

PORCELAIN CRAB: This crab can regrow a claw if one is hurt.

REMORA: Remoras are also called suckerfish because of the suckerlike organs they use to attach to other sea creatures.

SEA CUCUMBER: The deep-sea cucumber crawls along the ocean floor, eating what it finds.

SHARK: The whale shark is the largest fish in the world.

SHARP-FANGED EELS: Eels have long, slender bodies like snakes.

SPOON WORM: The spoon worm hides its body between rocks. The male is parasitic on the female.

WARTY FROGFISH: This fish is also known as the clown frogfish. It looks like it is covered with warts.

WHALE: Gray whales are often covered with barnacles that make their backs look like crusty rocks.

FIND OUT WHAT HAPPENS IN THE NEXT . . .

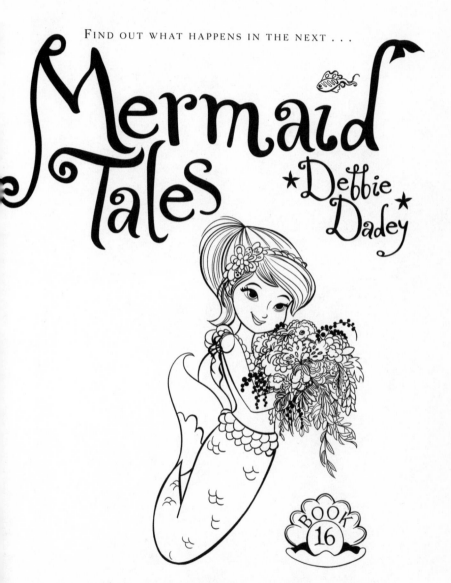

Mermaid Tales

★ Debbie Dadey ★

BOOK 16

Flower Girl Dreams

Splash-a-riffic

ISN'T THAT THE MOST FIN-TASTIC purse ever?" Pearl Swamp squealed. She pointed to the cover of a *Mer-Style* magazine with her gold tail fin.

Her best friend, Wanda Slug, moved closer to see the adorable scotch bonnet shell purse. "Ooh, I'm going to ask for one of those for my birthday!" Wanda exclaimed. "I wonder if it comes in pink?"

"Hey, watch out!" Pearl snapped as another third-grade student bumped into her, causing her to drop the magazine.

"Sorry, but I can't be late to class again," Rocky Ridge said. "Or Mrs. Karp will make me shark bait!"

Pearl shook her head and watched Rocky zoom across the huge entrance hall of their school, Trident Academy. He zipped between some chatting sixth graders and a group of fourth graders tossing a puffer-fish ball. It was still a few minutes before school started, and it was unusual for Rocky to hurry to class.

"That Rocky is so rude sometimes,"

Wanda said, scooping up the magazine and handing it to Pearl. "But he's kind of cute, too."

Pearl giggled. As she turned back to *MerStyle*, she overheard something that made her tail spin. She swirled around to listen to a group of mergirls from her class.

"I can't believe the wedding is in less than one week!" Kiki Coral squealed.

"Who's getting married?" Pearl whispered to Wanda.

Wanda shrugged. "I don't know, but weddings are wave-tastic! I was a flower girl in my cousin Detrella's wedding, and it was a splash."

Pearl sighed. She had always wanted to be a flower girl, ever since she'd attended her own cousin's wedding when she was a small fry. But so far, no one had asked her.

"Let's check with Kiki," Wanda told Pearl. "Maybe the bride is someone we know!"

Wanda swam up to Kiki and said, "We heard you talking about a wedding. Who in the great wide ocean is getting married?"

Pearl couldn't believe Kiki's answer!

Mr. Fangtooth's Surprise

MR. FANGTOOTH, THEIR school's grumpy cafeteria worker, was the last merperson in the ocean that Pearl expected to be getting married. Even though he had once saved Pearl from a great white shark, he was still the biggest grouch in Trident City.

After the conch bell sounded to start the school day, Pearl sat at her desk and thought, *Who would want to live the rest of their merlife with a cranky old merman?*

Before class began, Kiki had told Pearl that she, Echo, and their friend Shelly were going to be flower girls in Mr. Fangtooth's wedding. They would get to float down the aisle before the bride, carrying big bunches of flowers. They would probably wear beautiful gowns, too, and maybe even flower crowns. It wasn't fair that they were going to be in a wedding and Pearl was not!

"Today," Mrs. Karp told her third-grade class, "we will begin studying coral reefs. Tomorrow we will go on a short ocean trip to investigate the reef here in Trident City."

"Totally wavy!" Echo said.

Pearl smiled. School was okay, but it was a lot more fun to learn away from her desk. And she did like coral, especially the red coral that grew near the front door of her shell.

"There are both soft and hard corals," Mrs. Karp said. "Who can name a type of hard coral?"

Kiki raised her hand and said, "Brain coral?" She blew her nose into a kelp tissue.

"Very good," Mrs. Karp said. "Are you feeling all right, Kiki?"

Kiki nodded. "I'm allergic to paddle weed, which is blooming right now."

Pearl noticed Kiki's red nose. If Kiki was allergic to flowers, she definitely shouldn't be a flower girl.

There had to be a way for Pearl to be in Mr. Fangtooth's wedding too. After all, she was an expert on sea flowers. And she read every issue of *MerStyle* magazine from start to finish, especially the wedding articles. Plus, Pearl knew how to float with style.

Pearl smiled and made up her mind. She was going to figure out a way to be a flower girl in that wedding, if it was the last thing she did!

How to Be Nice

BY LUNCHTIME, PEARL HAD come up with a plan. If she was really nice to Mr. Fangtooth, he would surely ask her to be a flower girl in his wedding.

But Pearl had never been friendly to Mr. Fangtooth before. She *had* thanked him when he saved her from a shark in Trident Academy's dorm, but otherwise she tried to stay far away from him. After all, who wants to be around a grouch?

Pearl remembered that earlier in the school year Kiki, Shelly, and Echo had tried to make Mr. Fangtooth laugh with funny faces, but it had never worked. So Pearl wasn't exactly sure how to put her plan into action. After all, it was hard to be pleasant to someone who never smiled.

That was it! She would smile at him. As Mr. Fangtooth dished her favorite meal of black-lip oyster and sablefish stew into her shell bowl, Pearl flashed him a huge grin.

Mr. Fangtooth looked startled. He

frowned even more deeply. "Is something wrong with the food?" he asked.

"No," Pearl said. She showed all her teeth in the biggest smile she could muster.

"Then stop looking at me that way," Mr. Fangtooth grumbled. "You're giving me a headache."

Pearl's smile disappeared. "Well, of all the mean things to say!" she snapped, then slammed her mouth shut. She was trying to make him like her, and fussing wouldn't help.

Pearl sat down at her table and watched Mr. Fangtooth. He frowned at every merstudent in the food line . . . except for Echo. He actually *smiled* at Echo! What had Echo done to make him stop scowling? Pearl had to find out!

Debbie Dadey

is the author and coauthor of more than one hundred and sixty children's books, including the series The Adventures of the Bailey School Kids. A former teacher and librarian, Debbie and her family live in Sevierville, Tennessee. She hopes you'll visit www.debbiedadey.com for lots of mermaid fun.